Unchained Thrall

Alaric Maison

Published by Alaric Maison, 2023.

UNCHAINED THRALL

First edition. December 30, 2023.

Copyright © 2023 Alaric Maison.

ISBN: 979-8230229902

Written by Alaric Maison.

CHAPTER 1

Fingers dug into his back, as the man shuddered beneath him. The sign of yet another night ending exactly the way Aidan preferred.

"Aw, you're not staying?" Aidan leaned up against the couch, giving his living room an absentminded glance. That was as far as they got into his apartment earlier, before desperately needing each other.

The stranger was already standing up, getting his clothes back on.

"Mmh, I would love to. But then I'd never be able to get up in time for work."

"That good, huh?"

"...Maybe."

As his footsteps receded into the distance, Aidan soon heard the sound of his front door slamming shut.

He was alone again, lying satisfied on the sweaty couch cushions. Aidan reached over to the coffee table next to him, picking up his phone. With a smile, he placed it to his ear.

"Hold on... I'm not sure I like that you're calling me this late. Did you just ...?"

Aidan's grin grew at the sound of his friend's suspicious voice.

"You know me so well, Leo. Now, let me tell you exactly how it went."

Hearing the other's joking tone, Leo rolled his eyes.

"Oh, absolutely not. What did you actually call me for? I should be sleeping at this time. ...Like most people."

"Alright, alright. I just wanted to know if you'd like to hang out at the club next weekend?"

"Who would I be if I said no to that? As long as you don't run off with some guy after five minutes."

"I'll... uh... try."

"Unbelievable." Leo let out a huff.

"You love me."

"Somehow."

Despite all the loud and excited voices, obnoxiously loud music managed to drown it all out. Flashy stage lights shone from multiple directions of the club.

Aidan and Leo were making their way through the large crowds of people, looking for a place to sit down. To their dismay, the few couches that did exist were covered in unknown substances. Deciding against it, they went over to one of the place's many bar counters.

"I guess that wasn't out of the ordinary. Standing isn't so bad though."

Aidan stood fairly close to his friend, ensuring he could even hear him speak.

"Still... No bar stools either?"

Leo let out a short laugh at that, glancing at Aidan whose eyes were already scanning the garish club.

"Searching already?"

"No way, I would never..."

That immediately earned Aidan a raised eyebrow—but he didn't see it. All his attention was on something else. Leo followed his eyes, shaking his head when that question had been answered. The search was successful, it seemed. Aidan looked back at his friend again, giving him the most apologetic face he could muster.

"Please... You understand, right? I mean, look at him."

"...Yeah, okay. I see it. But you have to promise to stay by my side tomorrow."

"You're the best." With a grin, Aidan gave Leo a light pat on the shoulder. And into the crowd, he went.

"Well... I expected as much."

Aidan had no intent on letting this chance go. Their eye contact lingered the whole time. Aidan pushed past an absurd number of drunk partygoers until he finally ended up right in front of him.

"Couldn't help but notice your piercing gaze." Not to mention everything else.

"That a good or bad thing?" What a dangerous smile... They both knew exactly where this was going.

"Bad... How am I supposed to control myself when someone like you gives me that look." Adding to his words, Aidan ran his hand down the stranger's arm. He shivered at first, before grabbing Aidan by the shoulder with clear intent.

"Someone like me, huh? I wonder what that means."

That wasn't the usual response he got. But it was hard to deny the way it made his body react.

"Mmh... I'm sure you know."

They didn't need to say anything else. The tension spoke loud enough on its own.

It didn't take long for the two of them to head out of the club together.

"Oh no, wait. You're also ..." An issue arose that Aidan never would have expected to be confronting that night. Neither of them was even considering lying down.

"Ah, yeah. You don't mind, do you?"

Did he? He wasn't quite sure. But... Maybe it was worth trying out at least once.

"I've... uh... never done that. At all."

He got a surprisingly friendly grin in return.

"No need to worry about that. I'll go slow."

Alright, that's what he was supposed to be saying. Why was it turned so much on its head?

Cutting Aidan's thoughts short, the man pushed him down into the mattress. A new—but welcome—angle. Aidan swallowed, reaching up to get a light hold of his cheek.

"Well then... what are we waiting for?"

Lying there, Aidan was overwhelmed with way too many feelings. All he could do was gaze at the stranger, who was sitting on the edge of the bed.

He was in a bit of a daze, his face heated and his eyes glazed over.

"...Damn."

When Aidan uttered that, the man got up and looked down at him.

"I take it that was a good reaction?"

Flustered, Aiden didn't dare look at him. He glanced in any other possible direction, scratching at his temple.

"Don't you have someplace to go back to?"

A brief laugh came from the man.

"Sure, sure. Enjoy your little identity crisis."

Though their eyes met for a second—it didn't last long. The room went silent as his footsteps receded into the distance.

Aidan was alone with his thoughts, but he couldn't process them.

It didn't really feel that bad. Honestly, he kind of wished it had been more... rough. What even were these ridiculous considerations? It was time to sleep. Now.

The bar's calm atmosphere and dim lights perfectly contrasted with how energetic yesterday's location was. Aidan and Leo even found a place to sit down this time.

"Looking a bit distant there, Aidan. Something on your mind?"

"You know how I'm always the one... on top of the men I meet?"

"Oh no, what have I done." He may have sounded exasperated, but Leo still carried a faint smile.

"Haha, hold on. I promise I'll be quick. It's just... I kind of let the opposite happen with that guy."

Leo feigned a shocked reaction, holding his hand to his cheek.

"Daring, are we?"

Aidan glared at him.

"Hey, it's new to me."

With a chuckle, Leo let his arm fall down by his side, as he leaned back against their shared couch.

"I know, I know. To be fair, I am a little surprised. It never seemed like something you'd do."

"Right? Something else was interesting though. All I could think about afterward was how annoying his gentleness had been. I know he did it to be nice, but ..." As Aidan got swallowed up by his own thoughts, Leo watched on with widened eyes.

"I know a place."

Aidan froze when his friend suddenly spoke up.

"A... place?"

"From what I understand, you want something more rough, right?"

"Uh..." Aidan didn't humor his accusation, a hint of red on his features.

"I'll take that as a yes." He paused.

"So, I've been to this building in the city that specializes in many things... related to that."

Seeing the way Aidan perked up, he knew he was on the right track.

"Interested?"

"No, no. It's totally fine... Don't worry. All good."

Leo stared at him, as he kept vaguely denying the offer.

"I understand. Guess you won't be needing the address then." They both went quiet.

"...Please give it to me."

A smile spread across Leo's face—victorious.

"I'll send you a message later."

The evening continued, as the thought of such an interesting place seared itself into Aidan's mind. Who would he be able to meet there?

What Aidan saw when surprisingly heavy doors slammed shut behind him wasn't what he expected. As in, it didn't look anything out of the ordinary.

Welcoming staff members led Aidan to a locker room for storing valuables. Afterward, they guided him to a rather cozy-looking lounge area. Leo didn't give him much to go off of, but this wasn't quite what he had in mind. People were just hanging out on couches and chairs, as they chatted with each other.

When it came to the people themselves, it was only men. That was yet again nothing too surprising for Aidan since he regularly hung out in places like that.

Something did catch his attention though, which was a set of stairs that some guys were going down. A faint blue glow emanated from the downstairs area. Aidan felt almost pulled towards it, intrigued. He made it over there and peered into the darkness, where he saw a few people walking around.

Wondering how they were all disappearing, Aidan went down the narrow steps. His question was quickly answered. A large number of doors lined the halls, most of them closed. There were panels of light on the dark floor, and blue shone from behind the few doors that were open.

Behind them... very recognizable sounds. He had a pretty good guess as to what went on down here. This floor was matching his expectations a lot more. Of course, the relaxing lounge was a nice touch as well.

However, what he didn't see coming—until he was right in front of it—was yet another staircase. Curious, he looked through it. This time the glow was red. It didn't seem to come from any light panels like where he currently was, and the glow was much fainter.

Was this the area Leo wanted him to find?

Every time he took a step down, the stairs creaked. It was quiet between the two floors. When he knew that, Aidan was much more aware of the noise he was making. The further he descended, the more sounds could be heard, as they drowned out his own. Even louder moans than the ones above.

They were still muffled behind walls and heavy doors, but it was impossible not to hear. The halls were getting increasingly darker, only lit up by a red gleam coming from the open rooms.

Curiosity got the better of him. He had to know what made this floor different from the other one. As Aidan got closer to one of the closed doors, he heard an interesting sound. A sort of... crack.

Slowly pushing the thick door open, he was met with quite a sight. Two men; one of them bound to the wall. Scattered all across his body, were deep and long marks. They resided mostly on his chest and thighs, which were on full display. The one standing in front of him was a little more clothed, wearing some rather tight pants.

Speaking of him—the one with a whip in his hand—he certainly was... something. Aidan felt his face heat up just from looking at the man. The short black hair he clearly knew how to style, and those deep maroon eyes.

Still a bit dazed, Aidan gazed over at the restrained guy again. And without a shameful bone in his body, Aidan walked closer to him. He looked exhausted, unable to recognize that someone uninvited had arrived. The guy was just panting, as he watched Aiden.

"It looks so painful. This can... feel good?"

He seemed incapable of responding, but the other man absolutely had something to say.

"You must be new. Also, well... considering you just barged in when the door was already closed."

Aidan shuddered. What a voice.

"Uh..."

That man was easily able to hold strict eye contact with Aidan, which made his cheeks flare up. The red only deepened when his stern expression shifted into a smile.

"What you've done is worthy of punishment, wouldn't you say?"

Aidan was momentarily stunned, not able to look away from him. He was first taken out of his trance when the other guy shifted a bit, making his restraints creak.

"I-I..."

"Some other time, though. As you can see, we're busy."

Aidan hesitantly walked back toward the door, eyes never leaving the other.

"I'll... think about it." Aidan sounded unsure, but there was no doubt in his mind that he was coming back.

"Good. Don't worry about finding me. I'm a regular."

That was the last thing Aidan heard before he stepped outside and closed the door.

As he made it back through the dark hallways, he wasn't quite present or aware of anyone else. Even if they were to walk right by him. He didn't even notice that blue light panels now surrounded him until someone actually managed to attract his attention. The look he was giving Aidan could only mean one thing—knowing the location and all. When he thought about it, it would be a shame to leave without spending some proper time there.

When the man pushed the door next to them open, it didn't take more than a second for him to decide.

The trip was successful after all, and he even secured something rather interesting for his second visit.

CHAPTER 2

A few days had gone by, and it was once again time to go to that place. The sun went down a long time ago. But that didn't stop the inner city from lighting up so much, it could be mistaken for daylight. Venues of all kinds had their shiny signs outside and some windows were almost blinding to look through.

Aidan noticed a familiar person who was walking in his direction.

"Look at you. Out again so soon?"

"I should be asking you the same, Leo. Also... how did you even learn about such a place? Something I should know?"

Leo chuckled, giving him a dismissive pat on the shoulder.

"Obviously, I'm never telling you that. Let me have my secrets. ...So, is that why you're out?"

"Wouldn't you like to know?"

"... Thought so."

Aidan bumped his shoulder against Leo's.

"Hey, now. I have a good reason. If you saw him, you'd understand."

"Him, huh?"

Aidan sped up his pace.

"Uh, anyway, see you some other time."

Leo tried suppressing his laugh but was unsuccessful.

"I don't get to see you like this very often. At least let me tease you a little bit."

"Yeah, haha, that's great. Bye for now-!" Aidan hurried to get ahead of him.

"Have fun."

They shared a quick glance, but that was the last they saw of each other.

Aidan knew exactly where to go this time. He did consider whether to search for the same room or not since there was no guarantee he would be there.

He walked through those same dark hallways. As he did, he bumped his shoulder into someone else, who was walking in the opposite direction.

"Ah, sorry."

The man's voice made him look up. It had to be...

"Wait, is that... you?" The tension in his body was immediate. They were standing next to a somewhat open door that only vaguely outlined them. Aidan pushed it open, and yes—with more light on him—he could confirm it was the same man.

"Oh? Inviting me in?" He teased, knowing full well why Aidan did it.

"Uhm... hold on. Wait, no."

Getting a laugh in response, Aidan realized that that might have been a joke. But... it had to be all deep and smooth too. This man seemed to know himself and his effect on others well, his smug smile all too present.

"Getting my hopes up like that... how could you."

After the other time they met, Aidan could more quickly pick up on what he was alluding to.

"I wouldn't be against that though. ...Going inside with you, I mean."

The man walked into the enticing red room, its glow lighting up his broad frame.

"Are you sure you know exactly what that entails?"

Aidan looked inside, seeing a myriad of things he had never even considered in a sexual context.

"No, not at all. But I want to find out."

"My, how adventurous you are. I like it." He slammed the door shut.

"Cedric, by the way. You?"

A red tint spread across Aidan's face.

"Oh! Right. I'm Aidan."

"Well... Aidan. See anything that interests you?" Cedric gestured toward both a wardrobe and multiple shelves that hung on the wall next to the bed. He was curious about his first impression. Aidan gave the place a once-over, his eyes landing on a particularly large phallic object.

"More like what scares me. How would that even fit?"

Cedric chuckled, following Aidan's gaze.

"I mean, unless you really want to try, I'd suggest avoiding that one." Cedric reached his arm up to one of the shelves, taking down what looked like a ring.

"No need to tell me twice." Noticing what Cedric was holding, Aidan gave it a curious glance.

"Moving fast, huh? Marriage was never something I considered. But... if you want to..."

Cedric held the ring up to show its diameter. That wasn't going on anyone's finger.

"Haha, I'm sure we're both aware that this isn't a wedding ring."

"Aww... now you're the one getting my hopes up."

"Great, we're even then."

With a smile, Aidan took the black silicone from him.

"So, how do you plan on using this thing?"

"Since you're new, I thought it might be a good one to start with. It's pretty vanilla. Also ..."

A hand landed on Aidan's shoulder, making him freeze up. His eyes locked on Cedric's.

"...The way 'this thing' makes men so desperate for me."

Aidan nearly melted under his gaze. And how he spoke. And, well, everything.

"D- Desperate...?"

"You'll see." Cedric trailed his hand over Aidan's shoulder, fingers playing along his collarbone and the collar of his shirt. Aidan shivered, as he held the ring tighter to not drop it. When Cedric moved forward, he, in turn, stepped back. Both of them slowly made it to the large bed in the middle of the room.

As they got onto the edge of the bed, Cedric ran his hands down the other man's body. Aidan leaned into the touch. Just a single glance at Cedric's captivating smile, and Aidan was already willingly falling under his control.

Once Cedric made it to the rim of his shirt, he pulled it up, helping him out of it. Aidan didn't usually feel that exposed, but there was just something about being watched by that man.

"I expect you to take it off too..."

All he got in response was a chuckle, as Cedric shoved him down into the bed.

"Are you usually this flustered?"

Moving further back on the mattress, Aidan looked up at him.

"Not even a little bit. It's all your fault..."

"I would love to take credit for that, but I don't think that's all there is to it." Cedric grabbed the bottom of his own shirt—abiding by Aidan's request—he pulled it off and threw it on the floor.

"Maybe..." Aidan wanted to elaborate but trailed off when he saw Cedric both half-naked and on top of him. He did get a glimpse of it the first time they met, but this time it was entirely different. He did it for him. And he was... so close.

Cedric reached for one of the lower shelves, lined with only the most essential things. For example, the condom and bottle of lube that he picked up. Aidan quietly watched the other man, as said items were placed on the mattress next to him.

"Cedric."

"Hm?" Cedric's hands were already on Aidan's pants, lightly tugging at them.

"Who let you look that good?"

Cedric gave him an amused smile. He hooked Aidan's boxers under his fingers as well, before pulling both all the way off.

"Careful. Too many compliments and I may suddenly forget that you're a beginner."

In a twisted way, Aidan kind of wanted to be treated like the men he had been with before. The ones that knew how hard they wanted it.

"...And those beautiful dark brown eyes."

"Thin ice, Aidan. Thin ice." As he spoke, Cedric got the last of his own clothes off, only making his words seem even more sincere. He poured some of the lube onto his hand, but instead of slathering himself in it—he grasped Aidan's cock.

Aidan inhaled sharply.

"W- Wait, why on me-?"

"Just a little bit. It lets the ring more easily slide down."

Aidan glanced at the thing still in his hand, finally understanding what it might be used for. He held it over the head of his cock, seeing how well the size matched.

With a sly look, Cedric pressed down on Aidan's hand, pushing the ring down his cock. Managing to close his mouth in time, Aidan avoided making any noticeable sounds. It was close though.

"...I still don't know exactly what it does. But I'm guessing 'I'll see.'"

"Clever boy."

Aidan couldn't explain why that did something for him. Though, at that point, he was surprised by too many new things to worry about that particular one.

Getting more lube on his hand, Cedric coated himself in it this time. The condom followed soon after. There was still some liquid left on his hand, which he hovered between Aidan's thighs.

"Want me to go slow?" Cedric didn't move when he spoke, an action that was making Aidan more and more impatient.

"No... just... fuck me already."

The man's face and the way he said those words... it was impossible to deny what all that ignited in Cedric. When he finally pressed his fingers against Aidan's sensitive skin, it was with two, not one. Aidan took in a sharp breath—gasped—as Cedric made quick work of invading his body.

He pulled back out a little to let Aidan get used to the intrusion, before shoving them even further inside. Aidan held tightly onto the sheets, not expecting the aggression. It felt just as good as that other time. If not better.

...Okay, definitely better. And with much more technique. Especially when Cedric's index finger slid far enough in to scrape against the sensitive area that so easily made his whole body quiver.

He really did like this feeling; that much was becoming clear.

"Good enough. I don't think I can wait any longer..." Cedric pulled his hand out, leaving Aidan feeling more empty than he could handle. He watched as Cedric ripped open the condom's packaging, before rolling it down his cock.

"Cedric... h- hurry..."

Cedric chuckled, the sound of it making Aidan's cheeks heat up yet again. Why was that so hot to him?

"I could never say no to such a cute guy..."

Embarrassed, Aidan looked off to the side. Cedric made him feel way more exposed than any other man ever did.

Cedric guided his cock to where his hand was earlier, making Aidan tense up. As he slowly pushed himself inside, he got a good grip on the man's thighs.

"F- Fuck... So... tight." Trying to focus on the rousing way Aidan writhed, he had some slight difficulty getting all the way inside him. Despite needing some extra effort, the pressure on his cock felt good.

"Sounds to me like you're... ah... not trying hard enough..."

Cedric narrowed his eyes on Aidan and his shaky smile. He had way more confidence than Cedric was expecting.

"Oh, so that's how we're playing, huh?"

Cedric moved out a bit, only to thrust right back into him. Aidan convulsed from the sudden impact, as a wave of warmth spread throughout his body.

"I- I..."

"Where did your cockiness go?" He settled into a steady rhythm, both arms hooked securely around Aidan's legs. Aidan gripped the bed sheets even tighter, as Cedric grounded him into the mattress. His own moans and the occasional gasp kept him from responding immediately.

"I- It's- ah... still here... I promise..."

Nothing in Cedric's expression showed that he believed any of it; quite the opposite.

"For how long, I wonder?"

On cue, he shoved his cock far enough inside Aidan to hit that protruding spot he was aiming for. With a sharp inhale, Aidan's back arched visibly, as he tightened around Cedric.

"A- Agh-!" Aidan couldn't get more out, overwhelmed by the constant attacks against the same area. Cedric looked pleased but was unable to say anything witty with Aidan surrounding him so tightly. A familiar sensation stirred within both of them. But for Aidan, it was not nearly as prominent. He was starting to wonder why he wasn't getting closer when it felt as good as it did.

"I- I'm..." Cedric's sighs came out in tune with his thrusts, as the feeling got more intense. It didn't last long. His eyes closed, white flashing in his mind. His moans were much louder at that moment, as cum filled the inside of the condom.

He inched himself out of the squirming man below, before quickly disposing of the condom. The often-overlooked decision to place a trash can by the bed was a surprisingly great one.

Aidan didn't quite like where this was going. He gave Cedric a pleading look, as he whimpered from the unbearable emptiness.

"W- Wait..." Practically melting into the bed and panting heavily, Aidan reached for his own cock. However, a hand clasped around his wrist—stopping him.

"Did I say you could touch yourself?"

Aidan let out another whimper—conflicted. He was... getting edged. Wasn't he? It was something Aidan knew of, but he hadn't done it to anyone before. He didn't want to admit that the way Cedric exerted power over him was incredibly arousing.

"I- I should have been able to- I'm almost-"

"Maybe, and yet, you didn't come."

Aidan's hand was free. But, with such a strong presence in front of him, he wouldn't dare try to reach for himself again.

"With just a little more... I could ..." Still breathing heavily, Aidan sat up a bit.

"You'll need to deserve it first. How about..."

Aidan watched him with anticipation.

"Get on the floor."

CHAPTER 3

He didn't have to say that twice. Aidan would do so many things if it meant getting to come from this man's touch. Crawling off the bed, he got down on his knees. When Cedric sat down by the edge, Aidan settled in between his thighs. Cedric gave him a satisfied smile, cupping his cheek. So beautiful and desperate. Exactly how he loved it the most.

"Mmh... so obedient..." He slid his hand around the back of Aidan's head, before pressing those enticing lips against the underside of his cock.

"Cedric..."

"You know what to do... Put it in your mouth. If I'm pleased with your performance, I'll let you come."

Aidan swallowed hard, wrapping his hand tentatively around the man's shaft. And with his eyes locked on Cedric's, he trailed his tongue up the frenulum of his cock. He retracted it right as he reached Cedric's glans. He was so close to sliding his lips over him but didn't.

"Yes... sir."

Cedric shivered, his eyes widening. Aidan was striking just the right chord with him. He tightened his grip, and drove his fingers into the man's hair, pulling him closer. He forced Aidan to take him in his mouth, which he responded to by moving his whole body closer.

Cedric's legs trembled when he hit the back of Aidan's throat, enjoying the warmth that enveloped him. Aidan choked and had to pull away for a moment to catch his breath. Meanwhile, he got a good look at what was in front of him. That really was an impressive size.

"Nngh... so big. Sucking you off normally is going to be like deepthroating the whole time."

Cedric still let out a short laugh at that.

"Why, thank you... But, Aidan... that was another compliment."

In preparation for what he planned to do, Cedric scratched the soft skin of the other man's nape. And then—without further warning—roughly grabbed the back of Aidan's head and shoved his cock deep down his throat. Aidan made a loud choking sound, as tears gathered in the corners of his eyes. He expected that outcome, but not how vicious it was going to be.

It took some time to get used to since Cedric both moved Aidan's head, but also himself.

It was a new feeling to have his mouth filled up like that, unable to utter even a single word, and fucked as if he was a mere sex toy for Cedric to use.

What a thought... and a thrilling one at that.

"Fuck... you look good like that..."

The tone of Cedric's voice explained the amount of pre-cum that coated the inside of Aidan's mouth. Cedric felt his cock pulse, as he clutched the mattress with his free hand.

After a particularly needy thrust, Aidan pulled back in surprise. Opaque liquid scattered on his chin and trickled down his neck. As Aidan shakily held onto Cedric's thigh, the room filled with the sounds of their panting. Cedric watched him with hooded eyes and a soft smile.

"So brave... you were quick to hand over all your control to me."

Aidan ran his tongue over the cum that was still on the side of his mouth, swallowing it.

"I could tell you knew what you were doing."

"Good thinking." Cedric drove his thumb over Aidan's neck, gathering the rest.

"...So. Should I let you have what you've been waiting for?" He pressed his finger against Aidan's tongue, letting the liquid slide down his throat. Aidan's brows drew together, eyes locked on Cedric.

"Please..."

Cedric pulled his thumb back out and patted his own thigh.

"Get up here then." He moved back on the bed, legs still draped over the edge. A tense Aidan climbed onto Cedric, straddling him.

Getting a closer look at Aidan, Cedric noticed a darker color speckled across the bridge of his nose and cheeks.

"Huh... I didn't notice your freckles until now. It's my first time seeing that on someone with brown hair. ...Hot."

"Haha, uh... you know... you'd be very hot too if you touched me more..."

Cedric chuckled. He trailed his hand slowly along Aidan's leg until he reached his ass. Digging his fingers into the man's skin, he forced him closer; their bodies pressed together. Aidan's hand lay trembling on Cedric's shoulder, as he shifted against him in desperation.

"H- Hurry..."

Cedric swallowed hard. Though he wanted to tease him for longer, it wasn't possible anymore. He wrapped his fingers around Aidan's cock, his legs twitching from the sudden sensation. Finally being touched again, Aidan instinctively rocked his hips against Cedric's hand. The warmth of his palm was comforting in a way since Aidan knew he'd finally be able to come.

Cedric had a strong grip, his strokes speeding up over time. Feeling incredibly pent up, Aidan had to bury his face into Cedric's shoulder to muffle himself. He was already really close, and that was very much showing.

"Let go... Come for me."

That made Aidan's body flare up, and his eyes shut tightly. He didn't have time to process how much better Cedric's words made his touch feel. Aidan's breath hitched high in his throat. He shuddered against Cedric, as the familiar opaque liquid spread over his and the other man's abdomen. Aidan's eyes were watering, his moans both shaky and weak.

Cedric smiled, satisfied with the result and the drained guy who clung to him for support. He grabbed a rag off the shelf and drove it over his stomach and Aidan's, cleaning them both off. Afterward, he threw it to the side. He looked at Aidan the entire time, wanting to make sure he was okay.

Aidan's head fell onto Cedric's shoulder, his face nestled into his neck. Exhaustion was creeping in. But damn was it worth it. Cedric's hand was still on his cock, carefully pulling the ring off.

"How do you feel, Aidan?" His voice was a lot softer, as he rubbed the back of Aidan's head.

"Good... really good. But I want... more."

Aidan was surprised he let his honest thoughts out. He didn't even know what 'more' was supposed to mean.

Cedric chuckled, pulling his hand back. The end of the night was getting closer and Aidan already missed his touch.

"Getting a taste for it, huh? I'm going to like you."

With his cheeks a deep red, Aidan got off Cedric's lap and stood up in front of him.

"Ah, what is it with you?"

"Tell me, what did I do?"

His knowing smile really made Aidan want to retort, but at the same time, that face was also the reason he couldn't.

"You... ugh... What's your number?"

Cedric had to laugh, finding the state he was in quite amusing.

"Avoiding the question?" He stood up, making their height difference very apparent.

"What a bad boy."

Under that ever-so-watchful gaze, Aidan felt way too exposed.

"Just... say it."

"And now we're giving demands? Next time, you're absolutely getting... 'more.'"

"Nnh... You said next time. I'll need it if we're doing this again."

"Ah, got me there. I suppose you're right."

As they got their clothes on again, Cedric said the numbers out loud. Aidan's phone was in the locker, which was most likely why—Cedric the regular—didn't ask for it. He needed to remember what he said, so getting dressed was done in a hurry.

He had to say it over and over in his head, and once they were done, Aidan walked up to the door with haste. Of course, not without a longing look back at the man who was still standing by the bed.

"I'm expecting something rougher when we meet again."

Cedric glanced at him. He did enjoy that Aidan knew how to play cocky with him.

"You're not dodging all responsibility here. I'll be expecting a reason to do so. ...Continue acting like that though, and you might get what you want."

Just the anticipation of what Cedric's words might mean was making Aidan shiver; in the best way possible.

"I can't wait." Aidan flashed him a brief smile, before slipping out through the door.

Back out on the street again, Aidan took in the cold fresh air. It was a nice contrast from all the heat and sweat from earlier. Thinking back on it, it was easy to remember why he had some difficulty walking. That was a consequence he didn't mind so much, considering how great Cedric had been.

Though the inner city was as lively as ever, he knew it was late. And he'd rather not find out what the time was. Much of the city's activity came from sounds and lights that were further away from him. The more distant path he was walking on felt eerily quiet. Being aware of his own breathing and footsteps was making him much more anxious.

He always lived in bigger cities like this, so memories of the past were bound to come back. Especially when he was alone with his thoughts. Streets like these, with alleyways that seemingly went on forever. And the watching eyes of the people that inhabited them at night. They saw everything. What Aidan did was never hidden from them. And they hated it. Though his memories got more blurry as time went on, he could still feel them.

A chill ran down his spine. What if they knew what he had done? Were there any visible marks that he couldn't cover up? Was the way he walked too obvious? It was all too much. He had to get home.

With his heartbeat quickening, Aidan decided on running the rest of the way home. The mild pain didn't stop him.

CHAPTER 4

A few days later.

Aidan's thumb hovered over the bright screen and the list of names or phrases that filled it. A contact list with very few actual names, those being the ones closest to him. The rest were just short descriptions of people in a mostly sexual context. 'Freckled dick. Nice.' He remembered being a little envious of that guy. That didn't stop him from calling him again though, to get another glimpse at what he could have had.

The one he was currently hovering over was an encounter he bothered putting a name to. Cedric. A reminder of who he was or how it went wasn't necessary, as those letters did enough to give him a full-on flashback. He couldn't press it yet. He needed to let out his thoughts in some way. Scrolling further down, he saw the one that made the most sense—and clicked on his name.

"Leoo... my favorite..."

He heard an audible sigh from the other end, along with a chuckle that Leo was trying to conceal.

"Your favorite, what?"

"Uh... everything?"

"Fair enough. I love you too, or whatever."

Aidan leaned against his phone with a smile, as he simultaneously moved further back on the couch.

"You may say it like that, but I know you mean it. Deep down."

"Alright, no more of that. Reason for calling me this time?"

Aidan's face heated up a bit. A reaction he didn't expect. He usually talked to Leo about these things all the time, but right now it felt different.

"So... you know how I went there again?"

"Uh-huh."

The very subtle laugh alerted Aidan; Leo knew exactly where it was headed. Aidan's shaky voice was probably giving it away.

"I think I actually enjoy being... very... submissive. Or... uh... I did. I did enjoy it."

"You don't say. I think we've both reached that conclusion already. Anything else you want to add to that confession?" Aidan sighed. His friend was quick.

"I kind of want to experiment more with it. See if I can go further. And that guy..."

"That guy again, hm?"

"Right. The one I did it with... I think he'll be able to do exactly what I want..." He paused.

"He's so good, Leo. I don't know what to do with myself."

"Oh, how the mighty have... fallen? It's good though, to discover things about yourself. I hope you know I thoroughly enjoy watching you go through this."

"You're so mean."

Hearing Aidan's joking tone, Leo couldn't help but chuckle.

"All I'll say is, why not see where this leads? I would if I were you."

Aidan went quiet. He had to take a moment to appreciate that he was sitting there, talking to someone very important to him. One who bothered to listen to these things, and took them seriously. Despite some lighthearted teasing, of course. It was something to be grateful for.

"Yeah... of course."

Leo held his phone closer.

"You okay? Your voice... Did you lose focus? I can repeat myself."

"No, no. It's fine. I heard you. Just... uh... thank you."

Now it was Leo's turn to go quiet. That was a very general thanks, not directed at anything specific.

"You too. Don't forget yourself."

"I'll try. Bye, Leo."

"Bye ...my favorite."

As they hung up, Aidan smiled to himself, letting his head fall back. Calling him went great, as always. With a smile, Aidan got himself off the couch. The living room he was looking at didn't seem like much. It was mostly lamps and a television. And his couch, of course. He liked the simplicity. It felt especially calming today since the other apartments were quiet. Some of his neighbors had to be out for it to be so devoid of sound.

Scrolling back up on his phone, Aidan found the one he originally meant to call. He headed for the bedroom, as he tapped on the screen.

"Who is it?" A cautious tone.

Aidan had to wonder what type of person usually called Cedric for him to be answering like that. But damn, his voice was just as deep and smooth as he remembered.

"It's Aidan. If... you remember who that is."

"Haha, how could I not?" Luckily, Cedric sounded a lot more comfortable when Aidan was the one responding.

"You demon. You somehow got into my dreams. Only for a second though..."

Oh. Aidan didn't expect to hear that.

"I've been told I'm hard to forget. It's not surprising."

"Ahah, right. ...You thought of me too, didn't you?"

Flustered by the sudden accusation, Aidan sat down on the bed with a huff.

"Where's your evidence?"

"Your moans and the things you said to me. That made it pretty clear. I had a feeling I knew where your mind was going to be for a while."

Now Aidan's face was truly heating up.

"...Fuck you."

Cedric laughed.

"No need to be embarrassed. It was hot. And knowing you thought of me is... nice." He spoke so softly. It was starting to really get to Aidan, who pressed himself back against the headboard of the bed.

"So, did you call to plan something with me?" Cedric noticed he wasn't responding as quickly as he had been.

"Aidan?"

"Oh, right. Yeah. Would you want to meet up tomorrow? Or the day after?"

Cedric was getting more and more suspicious. Aidan's tone didn't match what he was saying.

"Tomorrow is fine. There are some nice cafés and such near the place we met. Near the place I... fucked you."

"Nngh..." Aidan swallowed.

"I knew it."

He writhed against the bedsheets he was desperately clutching and pressing against his crotch.

"You're aroused. And all I did was talk."

Aidan inhaled deeply, trying to get himself under control. He could tell Cedric was intentionally dragging each word out. He knew exactly how to get Aidan into this state.

"I don't know if you came from heaven or hell at this point."

"I think I'd prefer hell."

"Sounds about right."

"Alright, alright. Are we doing it? I'll just meet you at the entrance, then we can walk from there."

"Yeah... let's do it."

"Perfect. See you there, Aidan."

Just hearing his own name in this state was enough to send a shiver down his spine.

"See you..."

Right before they hung up, a laugh from the other end cemented itself into Aidan's mind.

"...What is he doing to me?" Though Aidan was clutching the bed sheets to hide his arousal from, well—no one—it was gaining a new purpose. More deliberately, he felt around in the soft fabric to find what was making his pants feel so tight.

"I can't believe I'm already doing this... it was just once. And a phone call."

He might be a little embarrassed by it, but he wasn't stopping.

The sun was starting to set. A familiar shadow leaned against the building wall, backlit by the sun. A black turtleneck covered by a gray jacket and dark suit pants.

It wasn't a bad look. Aidan felt a bit underdressed in his sweatshirt now.

"Do you always look that good intentionally, or were you born with it?" Aidan meant to say it in a spiteful way but realized how much that sounded like a line.

"Getting right to it, huh? No hello or anything?"

"Don't act like you didn't enjoy that."

"Perhaps... but you know where those words lead you."

"Good."

Cedric narrowed his eyes, surprised by how assertive Aidan was being.

"I swear... If we weren't in public right now..." He pushed himself off the wall, a dark red tint on his cheeks. With a smile, Aidan gestured to the lively street. Aidan was pleased to have gotten some payback after the phone call. With a smile, he gestured to the lively street.

"Shall we go?"

Cedric inhaled deeply.

"Yes."

As they walked, Aidan shuffled through different questions in his mind. There was just something about this person that intrigued him.

"I understand if it's not very exciting to be asked, but what do you do? You know, for work."

Aidan swore he saw a scowl on Cedric's face. But only for a moment. Honestly, that would be his reaction too. He just wanted to keep the conversation neutral since they were out among others.

"It's really nothing interesting. I work at a nightclub doing pretty basic tasks. Like... cleaning."

"I mean, hey, if it pays the bills. I work at a convenience store so it's pretty similar for me."

Cedric quietly studied Aidan's expression, searching for... something.

"Don't you wish you could do more? Be more?"

Aidan was a little taken aback by that question.

"...I'm guessing it's not just work you're talking about. I used to feel that pressure a lot. I'm still reminded of it at times. That I failed at most things that came second nature to everyone I knew."

"But you're okay with it now?"

"Mostly. I enjoy everything I do. Even if it's not something to proudly tell your family about. I don't regret a thing."

Cedric was looking quite enthralled, still not saying anything when Aidan finished talking.

"Cedric?"

A brief hand on his arm broke him out of it. He glanced off to the side where a thin alley stretched into the darkness between tall buildings. He grabbed Aidan's wrist and pulled him into the depths.

Aidan didn't have time to react before he was shoved against the cold brick wall. He looked up to see a flustered Cedric towering above him. The visual and somewhat surprising scenario was enough to make his face flare up as well.

"...That was weirdly attractive."

"What I... said?"

"...Kind of. And the way you carry yourself." Cedric moved his hand up from Aidan's shoulder to his neck.

"I don't know why exactly. ...I'll have to think about that."

Aidan laughed, placing his hand on the one trailing over his skin. However, when Cedric's lips brushed against his ear, he froze, aware of their location.

"Not... out here." That wasn't just Aidan not being an exhibitionist; acting like he didn't want to be seen. Cedric could tell that that was the case from how the man trembled and pulled away. He smiled, letting go of Aidan's neck when the grip on his hand tightened.

"Back to a more comfortable place?"

Despite his worries, Aidan was still very riled up from everything Cedric did. Even just being near him.

"Yes... please."

When would Aidan ever need cafés and awkward conversation when he could spend that time having someone like Cedric utterly destroy him. There was nothing else that mattered anymore right now.

CHAPTER 5

The room was as dark and intimidating as ever. But it was comforting in a way. Now that Aidan had gotten more accustomed to the place, his first thought was to look for something at least vaguely familiar. A metallic gleam on one of the shelves caught his eye.

More so did the item next to it, which looked similar in function, but was black and made out of leather. There were two sets on display.

"Now, these I recognize."

Cedric walked up behind Aidan, whose attention was glued to the shelf. He ran his fingers softly over Aidan's wrist.

"Ah, good old handcuffs. You're right to get distracted by those."

Aidan shivered at such a light touch, turning his head to look at the culprit.

"It would be a shame to ignore them."

As Cedric reached for both sets of leather cuffs, his chest pressed against Aidan's back. Both men went quiet. Getting confirmation of the close proximity they had to each other was making their breathing more manual.

"I take it you want to try...?" Though he lingered for a moment, Cedric managed to take a step back.

He walked to the bed's headboard, as Aidan merely nodded in response. He watched Cedric efficiently clasp each pair to their own bedpost. Sitting down on the bed, Cedric beckoned with his hand for Aidan to join him.

"Come over here."

A cocky grin spread across Aidan's lips, as he took a slow and short step closer to the bed.

"...What if I don't?"

"Come."

He froze. Cedric's commanding voice was enough to make that happen. And now it was getting irritatingly tight in those pants of his.

"Uh... yes, sir."

Aidan crawled onto the mattress, letting Cedric pull his sweatshirt off.

"Your shirt hides your form way too well." His hands moved down Aidan's body, tracing the ridges of his abs, before pushing him down onto the soft bed.

"Mmh... well... I don't show off as much as you do."

Cedric's fingers stopped short of Aidan's pants, as his eyes narrowed.

"Am I being judged right now?"

"Maybe. Uhm, I mean, I'm just calling you confident."

"Hmm..."

"You have good reason to be."

Cedric found his attempts at back-pedaling amusing.

"Alright, I suppose you saved it. Sort of."

Though the words were meant to calm him, Aidan didn't get much time to breathe. Cedric harshly grabbed his shoulder, moving him onto his chest; the side of his face pressed against the pillows.

Finally. That was all Aidan could think, as Cedric wrapped the black leather around each of his wrists. It was impossible not to want to try them—to pull his arms back and test their strength.

"Like it?" Cedric spoke in a hushed tone, freeing himself of his turtleneck.

"I... uh... yes..."

The whole scenario was overwhelming to Aidan's senses. His inability to move properly. And the half-naked man on top of him, who was currently taking what looked like a whip from the shelf.

Aidan's body kept getting warmer, as he watched Cedric run his fingers through the many tails of the toy.

"A pretty flogger, isn't it? Leather too, of course."

Aidan didn't even consider admiring its design when he was more occupied with thoughts of what it was capable of. And when those strips trailed up his spine, the anticipation only accelerated. He shuddered, pushing his face deeper into the pillows.

"It's... intimidating."

"Not in a bad way, I hope."

When it lightly brushed against Aidan's jaw, a faint smile crept onto his face.

"Never... unless that's a good thing."

Cedric chuckled.

"Well... bad and good—that can get complex. As long as you're into it."

"Oh, I am..."

When Aidan couldn't feel the flogger on his skin anymore, his eyes instinctively closed. His breath hitched, a surging feeling rising in Aidan's stomach.

"Good."

With no more than one word, he lashed the leather into Aidan's back. He gasped, his body shuddering visibly from the impact.

"A- Agh-!"

The area it hit was searing, but the pain didn't last forever, replaced with a sensation he couldn't quite describe. One that mixed with the warmth spreading inside him.

"Ah, a nice reaction... Enjoyed that, did you?"

Aidan opened his eyes, but only halfway, his cheeks and ears a dark red.

"Again... harder."

Cedric felt blood rush right down to his cock. What a sight.

"...If only you knew what you were doing to me." With much more force this time, Cedric whipped the flogger against Aidan's lower back. Aidan yelped, writhing and pulling hard at his restraints. But they were sturdy, keeping him right where he was.

However, having nothing to hold his legs down, Aidan desperately ground his clothed cock against the mattress. He didn't get much time to try and please himself, as the red-hot pain of the tails practically branded him again.

Cedric's smile grew when he pulled his arm back and saw the distinct marks on Aidan's skin. And the whimper that followed the last one...

"A- Ah... Cedric... m- more..."

To Aidan's dismay, Cedric placed the flogger down next to him.

"Don't worry... that's not the last you'll see of it." Cedric wasted no time, as he got Aidan's pants off in two rough pulls. Aidan felt even more exposed like this. Everything was on display and he couldn't move in any way to hide himself. But there was some relief to be found when Cedric pulled his own off as well.

"I'm way too hard for that right now..." He took a bottle of lube from the lower shelf. After covering his fingers with it, he put it back. Grabbing Aidan's thigh with his clean hand, Cedric spread his legs out for easier access.

Cedric teased just around the rim, before slipping his fingers into the other man. Aidan quivered, a long-drawn-out moan leaving him. It felt almost too good to have—anything—inside him. It was brief though. Once Cedric had gotten to every area he felt he needed to, he pulled back out. Aidan whimpered. The emptiness was as usual; too much to handle. He suspected Cedric was intentionally teasing him.

"Please... I want to feel you... I need it."

The red hues on Cedric's face spread to his ears, as Aidan moved his body backwards as much as he could. His ass came close enough to press up against Cedric's cock.

Even though it would have been fun to watch Aidan squirm for longer, Cedric couldn't hold himself back anymore. Like the lube, condoms were very accessible from the bottom shelf. He opened one and rolled the rubber down his cock. Placing both hands on Aidan's thighs, he dug his fingers into the man's skin. Aidan let out a surprised moan, as he instinctively backed up to feel more of it. He could tell that that wasn't just to get a better grip. There was a certain strength to it that brought its own kind of pain. And Aidan reveled in it.

Cedric, enjoying the reaction, slowly forced himself inside. But the instant he hit as far as he could, he pulled out, before thrusting back in even deeper. A ruthless rhythm.

Aidan's eyes were watering, as his breath hitched multiple times in his throat. His lungs were betraying him. His sounds; erratic.

Cedric let go with one hand, before letting it come back as a sudden slam against Aidan's ass. His eyes shut tightly. The stinging pain only added to every consistent wave of pleasure that overwhelmed all his senses. It didn't take long for a familiar sensation to rise in him. One that made his cock pulse, as precum leaked onto the mattress below.

"I- I... I'm-!" He couldn't form any other discernible words before his body collapsed. With his eyes shut, all he saw was white. He inhaled shakily. A moan followed, as his cum colored the sheets.

But Cedric wasn't done.

"Nngh... how dare you. Don't you have enough self-control to wait for me?"

Aidan opened his eyes as much as he could, looking apologetically at Cedric.

"S- Sorry... How can I... make it up to you?"

Cedric swallowed, gripping his thighs tighter.

"You... demon." He shoved himself even faster into Aidan this time, as precum dribbled down his cock. The new sped-up pace was making Aidan tremble under his strength. Despite the fact that he just came, it still felt so good to be continuously violated without a single break.

Cedric could feel himself reaching the edge, his more frantic movements making that clear. Aidan was very slowly getting aroused again, right as a sudden and harsh thrust made him pull on the cuffs' chains. A moan escaped Cedric; louder than any sound Aidan had heard from him before. He was even trembling a bit more than usual, as he rode out the climax and slowly dragged himself out of Aidan.

"D- Don't-! Stay..." Aidan whimpered, writhing in an attempt to feel the texture of the bed against his cock.

"Someone came a little too early. ...I'll show you exactly how you can make it up to me." Cedric rolled the condom off, throwing it into the room's dedicated trash can. In the corners of Aidan's pleading eyes, his tears were drying up.

Cedric's smile merely widened, as he picked the flogger back up. Aidan was getting more and more impatient. But seeing what Cedric was holding was enough to fuel his hope again.

"This is the only thing that'll be touching you." Cedric got a good grasp on Aidan's left leg, kneading his fingers into his flushed bare thigh. Readying the shaky man below for what was to come, Cedric ran the velvet strips along his perineum. With labored breaths, Aidan's whole body tensed up.

"H... Hurry..."

Cedric chuckled, pulling it back for a few unbearable seconds, before lashing it across Aidan's ass. He yelped, an intense heat spreading from his reddened skin.

Aidan enjoyed it much more than he could have imagined, made visible by the precum that leaked out with every hit.

"Got what you wanted?" Cedric watched the display in front of him with hooded eyes and deeply red features.

"Y- Yes...!"

Aidan gasped from the vicious attack that followed, before biting down on the closest thing he could reach. His teeth went into the cover of one of the pillows.

Cedric turned the flogger around in his hand. And with a smile, shoved the handle deep inside Aidan. He breached the man's body with ease, as he pressed the tip against his prostate.

Aidan inhaled sharply, barely able to make a sound. He felt his mouth dry up. The intense surge in him was so unexpected, he couldn't process how much of an effect it had right away.

When it was pulled back out, a heated and drawn-out moan escaped him. It was hard for Aidan to move the way he wanted to. A new feeling was spreading throughout his body. Where was he even anymore? The red lights blurred in his vision like a lens refusing to focus.

All that filled him was pain and pleasure, as he convulsed in ecstasy. A thick liquid painted the mattress below. The sight was one Cedric wouldn't be forgetting any time soon. His hand traveled down to Aidan's cock, so he could help him ride it out properly.

"Damn..." He didn't know what else to say. Few looked that good when they came, but there was just something about the way Aidan moved. And the sounds he made...

After Cedric pulled his hand away, he placed the flogger back on the shelf. Aidan collapsed, still twitching after everything Cedric had done to him. He looked on with barely open eyes, as the other man unlocked the leather that bound him. His body was near impossible to move, so all he could do was study Cedric, who was placing the cuffs back and cleaning up from under Aidan's stomach.

Lastly, he got his pants back on and sat down beside Aidan. It took some self-control to not mention the bite marks on one of the pillows.

"I know what happened to you. It's alright... just relax." Cedric grabbed Aidan's shoulder and helped roll him around onto his back. Feeling Cedric's warm hands on his skin, Aidan was quick to cling to his arm and hold him close.

"Keep... speaking to me. Let me hear your voice..."

Cedric's lips curved up, as he placed his cheek atop Aidan's head.

"Of course. Sorry if it gets long-winded, but let me tell you about a scenario I can't seem to get out of my head." He paused.

"Imagine this... It's midnight. The moon shines over the cozy outdoor area of a beach restaurant. Stretches of sand and rolling waves. Only lit up by the dim orange light coming from inside the restaurant. There you sit, feeling the night breeze and eating some of the best food you've ever had. Or just a good pizza."

Aidan let out a soft sigh and nuzzled against Cedric's arm.

"That sounds... very calming.

"I've always wanted to go... But I never ended up doing it. I suppose I've been busy with work and enjoying my time here. ...It does seem like such a nice way to spend the night though."

With some of his strength returning, Aidan sat up close to Cedric. That didn't change their height difference much. His head was perfectly aligned with Cedric's neck, which he nestled into.

"Ah, now I kind of want to see that scene. You sold it too well."

"I should know how to at this point. I've spent some time figuring out how to describe it."

Aidan smiled, trailing his fingers across Cedric's chest. He let out a sigh at the touch, looking down at Aidan with faint heat in his gaze.

"I won't lie, when you sound like that I can't help but be entranced by everything you say."

"You're really into my voice, huh?"

"How could I not?"

Cedric chuckled, noticing how that simple action was enough to make Aidan's face even redder.

"...Do you feel more stable now?"

"Yeah. That was... something."

Cedric pressed himself back against the pillows, as Aidan's fingers softly traced his collarbone.

"Ah... It's a very natural reaction to what your body has gone through. Hopefully that wasn't too shocking."

Aidan had to think about that for a second.

"I... kind of liked it."

Cedric couldn't have been more pleased with a response like that.

"Well then, Aidan. I'd like to properly welcome you to this life."

Their eyes locked on each other.

"You're a perfect fit."

CHAPTER 6

The bright multicolored lights and loud booming music did nothing to distract Aidan from his own thoughts. His eyes were glued to the liquid in his glass that swayed in time with the bass.

"Soo... I got a dog. He's the cutest little husky." Leo, who had been letting him stay in his trance for a while, knew it was finally time to break the silence.

Luckily, it worked. Sort of. Aidan glanced at the one sitting next to him, eyes faintly glazed over. The stiff couch wasn't easy to get comfortable on, but he tried his best to lean back on it. He placed the drink down on the table in front of them, a very soft smile on his lips.

"Oh, really? You've got to show me sometime. They're so... cute..."

Leo could tell he was drifting off again and had to speak up once more.

"Haha, right? Such lovely creatures. I could be convinced to let you see him."

"Nice... that's nice..."

That wasn't enough.

"Alright, how thoroughly did he ravage you? I've never seen you this spaced out before."

Aidan's eyes widened.

"L- Leo-"

Leo couldn't help but laugh, as he placed a hand on Aidan's shoulder.

"Hey, I doubt there's a better way to get your attention."

"You're an evil man."

Leo just smiled, waiting patiently for an answer to his question.

"We met up a few days ago. But I can still feel it, Leo. Everything." He paused.

"I thought I knew what sex was. Now... It's like I'm discovering it for the first time again. I want to learn more about Cedric's life. I want to be in it."

Leo watched him carefully, the smile never leaving his face.

"I'll admit, I'm starting to feel pretty proud of myself for giving you that address."

"Haha... you're the best."

Aidan looked absentmindedly around the club. A shadow that was moving in the distance immediately caught his attention. Tall and black-haired. The man wore a dark vest over his white dress shirt, as he walked along the back wall. Some other eyes were on him, but his reaction to them was a polite wave of his hand.

Leo was beginning to wonder why Aidan was being silent again. But when he followed the direction of his stare, he quickly understood the situation.

"Okay... that guy is pretty hot. But do you have to get all speechless like that?"

The man headed into what seemed like a staff-only back area. Did he work here?

Aidan was first able to speak up when he disappeared. He heard none of what Leo said.

"Huh... Cedric did say he worked at a club. There aren't many of 'these', so it makes sense he'd be here."

"Wait. That was him?"

Aidan wasn't sure why, but making eye contact with Leo was a little harder at that moment.

"Ah... yeah..."

Leo got up from the couch, patting the top of Aidan's head with a grin.

"Well, tell me how it goes."

"You..."

...And he was gone. It was too late to get Leo back now. A smug expression looked back at Aidan, as it was swallowed up by a mass of dancing shadows.

Squinting his eyes, he could just barely see Leo in there. He was already grinding up against one of the other men. Okay, that was probably deserved. Considering what happened last time.

He kind of wanted to go look for Cedric, but he was still a bit overwhelmed with his own thoughts. He needed time to process them. Besides, Cedric was still somewhere customers weren't allowed. It would be for the best to head home.

But that wasn't without a quick glance at his friend, easily discernible in the crowd with his blond hair. The flushed grin on his face was apparent. It was one that without fault made Aidan smile to himself. It was an indescribable feeling. Leo really did deserve the world.

He trusts me enough to let me into his apartment...

Aidan was beaming after yet another phone call. This time they planned for him to visit Cedric, which was quite an exciting prospect. Standing in his bedroom, Aidan looked through the closet for what to wear. The spontaneity of meeting him on the same day as it was discussed would normally be a bit stressful.

But Aidan already missed being in the same room as him. If anything, he would be out the door in a heartbeat, had they not agreed on a later time.

Reminded of when he saw Cedric at the club, he picked out a dress shirt. It would be a nice thought, and Aidan also wanted an excuse to try and look more formal.

He might have gotten a little too excited and prepared himself earlier than necessary. This was going to be a long few hours.

As he entered the apartment building, its dim lights didn't do much to calm him. It was an unfamiliar and dark stairway that momentarily made him forget what he was doing there. He sped up his pace. The address was only a few floors up.

Once he stood before the door with the correct numbers on it, he took a deep breath. As his fist hit the wood, muffled footsteps from behind the door soon followed. His unease faded quickly when he came face to face with the man inside.

A warm glow came from Cedric's apartment, as he stood there in the most closely fitted sweatshirt Aidan had ever seen. It looked like they might have had the same thought of mimicking each other.

Aidan meant to say something. He really did. But he was much more fascinated by how a thick shirt like that was able to hug Cedric's body so well.

"Aidan, please. Close your mouth, you're drooling."

Aidan perked up at that.

"Wait, my mouth isn't even o- oh."

Cedric laughed.

"I don't know... If it went on for any longer, that might have been the case."

Aidan stepped in through the entrance, locking the door after him. A perfect way to regain some composure.

However, that washed away the instant he turned back to Cedric, who was much closer now. He ran a few fingers down Aidan's chest, showing that he had indeed noticed his shirt was a bit more open than usual.

"Uh... lovely white walls you have here. Why don't we have a look at the rest too?"

Cedric pressed his hand harder against Aidan, making his back hit the door.

"Acting coy now, are we? ...Still riled up from last time?"

Why did he have to be so damn perceptive. Unless of course, Aidan was making it more obvious than he thought.

"Maybe..."

"Alright, I'll be nice. ...Until you start begging me for it, that is."

Aidan shivered, as Cedric pulled his hand back.

"You're pretty certain of that, huh?"

Cedric squinted his eyes.

"Yes. Yes, I am."

They both knew it was inevitable, but some playful defiance was to be expected. And since it had been established that they weren't ripping each other's clothes off by the door, Aidan could calm down a bit.

He slipped past Cedric. The entrance hall took a quick bend to the right and stretched out into a long hallway. There were four doors in that hall in total, two along each side. It was a rather small apartment, which Aidan could relate to.

"You know... ever since that time you got way too aroused in the middle of the street; just from me explaining myself. I've been thinking about what you said. And I really want to know more about you." Aidan opened the first door on the right. In there was a little kitchen with only the essentials and nothing more.

"Okay, back it up there, Aidan. I will not hear that from someone who got off to me just speaking over the phone."

"How dare you bring up such an embarrassing moment for me."

"Mhm... who started this again?"

Without looking back, Aidan hurried off to the next door. His living room; with a couch and television. What a familiar sight.

"Anyway! As I was also saying, I'm curious about you."

He didn't stay by that doorway for very long.

What about over here?

It seemed Aidan had finally found what he was looking for. The bedroom. As he stood in the doorway, Cedric walked up behind him.

"Well... I'm a little jaded." Cedric leaned down, placing his chin on Aidan's shoulder. He continued.

"I'm sure you can already imagine what in my past has led to it. You know, considering you're someone I met at 'that' place."

"If we're talking about childhood and teenage years, then yeah... I know exactly what you mean." Aidan reached his arm behind himself, placing a hand on the back of Cedric's head. He dug his fingers into his hair and kneaded gently. Cedric sighed against his neck, burrowing his face into it.

"Mmh... yeah. It sure was... something. But I think the more repressed I was, the better it felt to let myself indulge."

"There's definitely something to that. ...After all these years, I can finally do, well—this." Aidan rubbed even harder against the back of Cedric's head. That made him press his lips against Aidan's skin, muffling any sound that might escape.

"Also... thank you for being the first one I met in this part of the community. You gave me a good first impression..."

Cedric's mouth stayed on him, very slowly going up his neck. This time it was Aidan's turn to sigh, as Cedric grazed the edge of his ear.

"Nnh..."

When Cedric snuck a hand up under his shirt, Aidan's immediate reaction was to back up into him.

"You're welcome. I'm getting too much praise though... Or maybe I don't tell you how I feel often enough."

He enjoyed the way Aidan moved against him, as he explored every subtle curve of his body.

"Then, Cedric... be honest with me."

Cedric slid his hand in under the rim of Aidan's pants. However, he didn't go any further down than that...

"It may seem like I meet a lot of great men with the amount that come and go from that place. But... you're by far the best. Even the simplest things you do. They... start something in me." He retracted his hand from under Aidan's shirt and reached up to unbutton it instead.

"...In a way no one else has."

Aidan's cheeks and ears heated up significantly. He couldn't handle standing there anymore. It was time to move on. Fast.

CHAPTER 7

As the last button was unfastened, he took a rushed step toward the bed. Cedric chuckled, his arms falling down by his sides. Aidan turned around to face him, soft sighs leaving him.

"...So. Do you have any of those toys here?"

Cedric found the embarrassment a bit endearing. Aidan was clearly not good at taking those kinds of compliments. But neither was he.

"No, sadly. I visit the red rooms so much, I've never really had to. They have everything right where I need it."

Aidan walked over to the bed, sitting down on the edge of it.

"Then you better know how to be just as rough with only your body."

Cedric's brow furrowed, as a confident grin spread across his face.

"Who let you give me that demanding tone." When Cedric made it to the bed as well, Aidan crawled further back—shoulders up against the headboard. His expression was just as sly.

"I don't see you doing anything to stop me."

Cedric opened the drawer of his nightstand, taking out lube and some packets.

"Yeah? That can certainly be arranged..."

Aidan slowly pulled his disheveled shirt off, gaining Cedric's full attention.

"Then get on top of me already."

With no hesitation, Cedric climbed onto the bed.

"Still ordering me around, huh?" Cedric's shirt was thrown off in haste. He lightly caressed Aidan's neck, before wrapping his hand around his throat. Though it was hard, Aidan swallowed.

"Nnh- C- Cedric..."

He pressed his thumb further into Aidan's skin, making him tremble in his grasp.

"For the record, I've lived awhile with sadistic tendencies and no tools to help me. This won't be a problem..."

With his voice stifled Aidan could only choke when the man's fingers tightened around his neck. Cedric's eyes traveled down Aidan's body, stopping at the very visible shape that was forming in his pants.

"How filthy... Getting off to this. I should be punishing you just for that..." Cedric pressed his knee against Aidan's crotch, making his body shudder from the sudden contact.

As Cedric continued to knead into him, Aidan gasped for air. Tears glistened in the corners of his eyes. Cedric noticed and loosened his grip a little. Aidan's breathing was getting shaky, his face a deep red.

"Yes... please... I deserve it."

Aidan reached his hands toward the other man, feeling up his chest. Cedric let out a soft sigh, pushing his body forward to lean into it. Letting go of Aidan's neck, he moved his hands somewhere a bit different and tore Aidan's pants off.

"Mmh... damn right." He got rid of his own as well, grabbing what he needed from the nightstand. It only took him a few seconds to roll the condom on and slick his cock in lube.

"I'm not loosening you up. I want to feel... all of you."

They locked eyes, their gazes more intense than ever.

With those words, Cedric huffed, before forcing himself deep inside Aidan. He went as far as he possibly could on his initial thrust, an action that made Aidan arch his back.

Aidan tensed up when he suddenly felt a set of teeth touch his neck. Cedric bit down near the base—where his skin was more resilient. Warmth quickly spread through Aidan's body. It didn't take long for the sharp pain to be replaced with that new pleasurable feeling he had come to know recently. It was something he didn't know he needed but was now absolutely essential.

"Nnh- Fuck..."

Cedric's lips curved up, still pressed against Aidan's sensitive flesh.

"You tightened around me... That can only mean I did something right." Cedric moved out a bit, only to push back in again. The head of his cock rammed up against the other man's prostate. Aidan's breath hitched in his throat, prolonged by Cedric biting down on the other side of his neck. He shuddered violently, his body writhing on the mattress and against Cedric, trying to feel every inch of him.

Aidan was desperately trying to gain as much as he could out of every single thrust, which was immensely satisfying for Cedric.

"Why are you... so goddamn good." With one of Cedric's hands sitting firmly on Aidan's thigh, the other reached up behind his head. Cedric got a good grip on his hair, before roughly yanking it down, as he ground into him again.

This time, not just Aidan's back but his whole body arched off the mattress. Yet another form of pain that Aidan reveled in.

He was getting close, and seeing the uncharacteristic way Cedric was trembling—so was he.

"Bite me... again-"

Aidan almost didn't get the whole sentence out, before Cedric's mouth was on him once more. That mixed with the hand in his hair was such a delightfully painful combination. All his senses were on fire, as Cedric continued to ruthlessly attack the deepest part of him.

"C- Cedric... I'm-!"

"Good... come for me."

That voice... and his words. Even if Aidan tried his best to contain himself, it wouldn't be physically possible.

A sharp intake of air, and an elating surge of pleasure. His fingers dug into the sheets when he came, trails of thick liquid drawing lines down his cock.

Cedric moved back, pulling out of him. His breathing was heavy, manual, and he had some slight trouble keeping eye contact with Aidan. All that filled the room was soft panting coming from both of them.

Cedric rolled the rubber off, and threw it into the trash can that he knew from experience should be kept there. He then leaned down in front of Aidan, head between his thighs. Aidan's eyes—though dazed—widened at the sight.

"Ah... looking good there..." Aidan chuckled, fatigue in his voice.

Cedric traced his tongue over Aidan's abs, cleaning up what had dribbled down there.

"Haha, thank you. ...This is as submissive as you'll ever see me."

"Aw, I'm enjoying the view though..."

With a smug smile, Cedric moved his lips over Aidan's shaft, swallowing down the last that remained. Aidan shivered.

"Don't forget to keep these mental images for later then..."

"Cedric... You better not be teasing me for getting off to your voice. Memories of you had a lot to do with it too. Also, there's no way you didn't do something similar."

Cedric went quiet, brushing his fingers over the marks on Aidan's neck.

"...No. You're projecting."

Aidan moved closer, enjoying the soft touch. Though it felt nice, he wasn't about to ignore that comment.

"You think touching there is going to distract me? Don't try to deny it."

Cedric glanced off to the side.

"Fine... maybe I did. But it was after our second time."

Cedric really had done the same, huh? Because of him. Just that thought was almost enough to make him aroused again.

"I knew it."

Cedric pressed more roughly on one of Aidan's marks, the pain from earlier resurfacing. His face burned up from the sensation.

"No, you didn't."

Aidan whined.

"Okay, no. But I had my suspicions."

Cedric chuckled, as Aidan pressed his body up against him.

"Well… either way, I don't regret it. I'll probably be able to do it for as long as I know you."

"How romantic."

"Oh, shut up."

They both laughed.

A few quiet hours went by. The two relaxed in each other's presence, forgetting the rest of the world for a time.

But… it had to come to an end eventually.

Both fully clothed, Aidan and Cedric walked together, all the way out the door and the apartment building. Saying goodbye was never pleasant, so they wanted as much time together as they could.

"Whenever you have time off and want to meet, please contact me."

"Of course, Aidan."

Cedric stepped closer, leaning in close enough to graze Aidan's ear with his lips.

"Have fun getting home with that ravaged body of yours."

With a noise of surprise, Aidan stumbled backward.

"Damn, you."

Cedric chuckled, walking back to the large door behind them.

"Until next time."

Aidan couldn't contain his smile; as much as he wanted to after that. They waved at one another before Cedric disappeared into the darkness.

Aidan looked around the quiet streets, turning to walk alongside the building's brick wall. He thought he heard mumbling coming from further away.

Sounds like that stood out in an otherwise silent street, which made Aidan feel tense. What if those people were close enough to… no. There was no way.

It came from the alley he could see in the distance. Knowing that, he slowed his pace down significantly. When he was only a few steps away, he looked around himself cautiously. No one was speaking anymore. That should have been a sign for him to leave.

But he didn't get enough time to think it through.

Once he made it to the alleyway, an arm reached out from the deep and pulled him in.

His back slammed against the brick wall, as six cold eyes glared back at him. Aidan was paralyzed, hands shaking by his side.

It was three guys around his age, their clothes dirty and roughed up. The one with his friends on both sides, had him pinned to the wall. His frown was evident, but it wasn't exactly anger he was exuding.

"Hah. Not even trying to keep it hidden anymore, eh? You people are disgusting."

Aidan's brows furrowed deeply. Not this... It had been so long, and yet, his memories came flooding back. It left him even more frozen, unable to react when the guy held a gleaming blade of metal up to his eye.

"If I messed your face up, would it even be possible for you to get laid?"

Aidan tried to steady himself, leaning back as far as he could. Their looks were icy, but so was his.

"You seem pretty aware of a stereotype, or problem... among 'my people'." Aidan managed to retort, but a chill still ran down his spine when the guy pushed his knife closer in response.

"What do you mean?"

"You tell me." Aidan's voice lowered into a growl.

"Are you saying what I fucking think you are?" He reeled his arm back. With a pose like that, he looked ready to strike.

With widened eyes, Aidan reached his hand out in an attempt to protect himself. But because of that, the edge of the blade dug into his palm. Aidan's mouth opened, but no sound came out. The sting was instant, he couldn't even scream.

The guy let go, and Aidan slumped against the wall, trying to hold himself up with its support on his back. He pulled his sleeve over the wound, as blood painted the white fabric red.

The one on the right was quick to speak up.

"Dude, why did you even touch him to begin with? Let's just leave this fucker here."

"Ew, yeah. You're right."

All three stared down at him with disdain, as they followed each other out of the alleyway.

Aidan was trying his best to process what had just happened. His past forced itself back and he didn't know how to react.

He waited until they were all completely out of sight, before heading out of there and in the direction he originally meant to go. His eyes were glazed, getting wetter as time passed.

CHAPTER 8

Aidan hoped sleeping on it would help, but by the next morning, he felt just as hollow.

He had been lucky for so many years; somehow avoided them. But... those very real people showed themselves to him again.

A grim reminder. Just like the wound he had to waste his first aid kit on. It wasn't as big as it felt, but it still hurt like hell back in that alley.

All his thoughts were starting to culminate in one person. Cedric. It happened after he had been a little more public with him. It would be impossible to see that man now. It was only going to bring the past back... right?

His concerns were already spiraling out of control, but there was no stopping it. Hiding had to be the single correct option.

A whole week slipped by. Aidan couldn't bring himself to contact anyone. Both Leo and Cedric kept trying to reach out to him, but he didn't respond to either of them.

It was around midday, and the streets were bustling with people. A perfect time for Aidan to get out and hide among them. All he needed was groceries, but he was still cautious of familiar faces.

However, much to his dismay, a pair of eyes met with his. When the person realized who was standing a short distance away, it was too late for Aidan to hide. And though he kept walking, Leo easily caught up to him.

"Explain yourself. You know I get concerned when you do things like this."

Aidan slumped his shoulders in defeat but didn't know how to reply. That only made Leo more worried.

"...I'll let you pet a dog while you tell me. As in... I'm inviting you over. I don't like that empty look. Something's up. And trust me, a husky helps."

Aidan looked down at the ground with a sigh. It took him a second, but then he nodded.

Since they were already walking, all that changed was a shift in direction.

It was a quiet and tense trek to Leo's house. They had to walk far outside the inner city to get there.

Once they walked through the fence that led to his garden, Aidan's expression lit up. A husky came bounding toward them the instant Leo closed the fence.

"Woah there, easy." Leo had to pull the dog by its collar, ensuring he didn't jump on Aidan. From the way it ran, that was very likely. As the dog was held back, Aidan moved his hand over the back of its head. The soft fur had a surprisingly calming effect on him.

He knelt down, coming face to face with Leo's excited canine. Its reaction was to try and lick his hands, which Aidan gladly let happen.

Leo's eyes narrowed on him, but he didn't say anything. He let go of the collar, seeing that his friend seemed to have calmed down the beast.

"So... want to tell me why you disappeared?"

Aidan didn't respond at first, purposefully not looking back at Leo. His body felt heavier than ever, but he still managed to stand up again.

"...It's impossible to escape them. I don't know what to do."

Though cryptic, they had known each other long enough for Leo to catch on.

"Oh... Oh no. Aidan..." He stepped closer and wrapped his arms around him. The husky perked up in surprise. Aidan reciprocated, holding his friend even tighter. He didn't expect it to feel that good to say something.

"I was going to mention the scar, but I'm sure you don't want to revisit that scene."

Just the word was enough to make Aidan's hand twitch.

"You ..."

"Ah, sorry."

Despite their words, the mood was still lightening up. Aidan couldn't have asked for a better person to be by his side.

"I won't bring it up again. Unless, of course, the exact details are important."

They both pulled away so they could see each other and the dog with his pleading eyes, who was trying to get their attention. Aidan ran his hand through its fur once again.

"Yeah... that's not important. I'm just not over that they're still everywhere. I was beginning to believe they didn't exist anymore."

"Most adults do tend to keep it to themselves compared to kids and teenagers." Leo paused, letting out a sigh.

"But... it's never really going to go away completely. The best we can do... is live. Whichever way that might be."

Aidan couldn't look away from him. He knew Leo's experience backed up his words.

"...Leo. You're the only person I'd hear that from, and take it seriously."

Leo's expression was unreadable, but his lips did curve up a bit.

"You give me too much credit sometimes."

Leo chuckled, giving Aidan a friendly pat on the shoulder. Why did Aidan feel like he was being told that a lot.

"It might be a lot, but it's well deserved."

Leo reached for Aidan's hand. The one combing through the dog's fur.

"Are you trying to make me fall for you? Cause it's working."

Aidan laughed. For the first time that week.

"Okay, now I've officially said too much. Can't have you seeing me differently all of a sudden."

"Haha, oh please, I could never date a fiend like you."

"Wow, I'm hurt."

Leo slowly shook his head with a smile.

"By the way, since you haven't been responding to me... what about that guy?"

Aidan looked away.

"...I might have given him the same treatment."

"Then I think you know exactly what to do now."

"Hold on. Let me stay here for today. I need to pet your dog more."

"Told you. He's a very helpful boy."

"I love him already..."

Maybe, just maybe, he was going to be alright.

It was dark and cold outside the restaurant. Only a faint glow came from behind the front windows. Aidan leaned against the wooden building, holding his phone up to view the message chain shining from its screen. It contained some pretty vague texts from him about meeting at some address. And a very confused Cedric. Even so, he hesitantly agreed to come see him.

There—in the distance—a familiar shadowy form came walking in Aidan's direction.

He had less of a gleam in his eyes than usual, which was to be expected. Distinguishing between whether he looked annoyed or concerned was tough. Though either were replaced with widened eyes once he saw what Aidan was standing outside of.

"Is this ...? I was wondering why you had me drive so far outside the city." When his eyes landed on Aidan again, he furrowed his brows.

"Wait, that's not what I want to ask. Where were you?"

Aidan intentionally avoided eye contact, a sinking feeling in his gut.

"Uh... thank you for coming, despite... you know."

Cedric sighed, somewhat irked by his evasiveness.

"I might not like that you disappeared, but I'm not just going to say no to seeing you again. I care about you."

Aidan looked up after hearing that.

"I- I really am sorry. I'll tell you why in a minute, just... let me lead you to our table first."

Cedric eyed him silently, before nodding.

Aidan guided him through the building, where a host showed them to the table that had been reserved for them.

It wasn't inside. The chill breeze swept through their hair, as the moon shone above the calm waves not far from them. People were strewn across the place, chatting with each other. The place looked incredibly close to how Cedric had imagined it.

As they sat down, he still couldn't take his eyes away from the view. The blue and orange combination was so captivating.

"I'll admit... this was rather nice of you."

Aidan cautiously watched him. Seeing Cedric so serene wasn't a common occurrence.

"I thought you might enjoy it. But yes, let me tell you what happened."

Aidan recounted everything that went on after they said goodbye that day.

"... It brought back a lot of things I'd rather forget."

The whole time Aidan was talking, Cedric had been rendered speechless.

"I... I should have walked you home or something... I..."

"No, don't blame yourself. It wasn't your fault. ...But I do appreciate the thought."

Though Cedric wanted to push it further, he understood and didn't try to refute it.

"...Where are they? I'll get them. ...Okay, I'm kidding. Surprising as it may sound, I'm not an aggressive asshole like them. That doesn't mean I'm not going to do anything if I see those people near you though."

"Hmm... you know... imagining you winning a fight against them is kind of enticing." Aidan had a faraway look. And Cedric couldn't conceal his smile, as he moved back on the chair.

"You might be a little more messed up than I thought."

"Alright... I'm also kidding. Kind of."

Cedric let out a short laugh.

"I prefer being aggressive... consensually."

"Ah, you don't say. Speaking of... all that. I've been wanting to get away from the city. Even more than just this restaurant. More secluded and for a longer time."

Cedric raised a brow, an amused smile on his lips.

"Oh? Is there a chance I'm involved in that plan?"

A red hue spread from Aidan's face to his ears.

"You... could be."

"Where are we going?"

"I was thinking of renting out a cabin of some kind for the weekend. Far away from all the noise. And people."

"That does sound nice... but I'm not letting you pay for all of it."

"No, no. I want to."

"At least let me handle half."

Aidan went quiet, his attention was fully captured by Cedric.

"...Okay. We'll split it."

"Perfect. Just like what we should be doing tonight, if you feel like calling the waiter over, that is."

"Cedric, please. I invited you out. Let me do it."

This time Cedric was the one who needed to think.

"This is the last time I'll let you do that."

"Hm? Worried our roles are being switched?" Aidan was joking, but the subtle way Cedric shivered made him a little suspicious.

"Wait, actually?"

"I... I can't help it. I've always been like that."

Aidan leaned over the table, eyes locked on Cedric's.

"Well... then let me be the one to tell you this. You don't have to be the leader. I can care for you too."

Cedric didn't know how to reply to that. Some cogs seemed to be turning from the look on his face.

"...Let's get something to eat, shall we?" There was a certain shakiness in his voice and some visible heat on his face.

Aidan just smiled. Based on the last time they had this kind of talk, he knew exactly what that meant.

"Yes."

Hidden behind an almost endless number of trees, stood a striking wooden cabin. It seemed to have been very well maintained. That much was clear.

The scent of wood was calming.

"You chose well, Aidan." Cedric walked toward the surprisingly ornate door, a large bag in his hand.

"It's pretty, huh? ...I can't wait to escape for a while." With a smile, Aidan moved up next to him. He had a bag as well, but his wasn't nearly as big.

"When you told me about the idea, I already saw it in my head. I could definitely use a weekend like this. But you especially."

Aidan slipped past him, unlocking the door with the key he had been given. That wasn't without a quick look at Cedric, of course.

"Yes. Make me forget... I know you're *very* capable of that."

Cedric chuckled. He knew exactly what Aidan was insinuating.

As they walked through the cabin, its cozy interior did wonders to make them feel at home. There weren't any big and obnoxious artificial lights, only smaller ones with a dim glow that almost made it look like candlelight.

They reached the living room, where Cedric placed his bag on the sofa table. When he did, his eyes drifted away from the other man. He moved his arms more carefully than usual, as he opened it. Aidan could tell something was up, but he didn't know what.

"Cedric?"

As he dug through the bag, he looked back at Aidan.

"So... I took something with me."

"Something that isn't an obscure sex toy?"

"Hmm... It could be used that way if you wanted to."

Aidan let his bag fall to the floor and peered over into Cedric's. What he was pulling out of it looked a lot like a collar of some sort. Black and made of leather. That seemed to be a favorite of Cedric's; or just what most looked like.

"Oh..."

With a soft smile, Cedric opened it.

"Do you... understand the significance of this?"

Aidan walked closer, placing his hands over Cedric's.

"I do... I've done my research."

Guiding Cedric's hands closer to himself, he let him wrap it around his neck.

"And yes... I want to."

Aidan watched him carefully, as Cedric closed the collar.

"Based on my experience with most things in life, I didn't know I had enough luck to meet someone like you." Cedric lingered by Aidan's shoulders and the base of his neck. He kneaded his fingers into Aidan's skin, earning an approving sigh in response.

"Mm... so sappy."

"Hey."

"Haha, I'm just not used to it. But thank you. I like this side of you too..." He rubbed Cedric's wrist with his thumb.

"I appreciate that. ...And don't worry, this isn't about to become a regular thing."

"I won't mind it once in a while." Aidan leaned in closer, his voice lowered to a whisper.

"But I much prefer it when you're fucking my brains out."

"Oh, Aidan. How vulgar."

"I know you love it."

Cedric slipped two fingers under the collar. And But I much prefer when you're fucking my brains out."

"Oh, Aidan. How vulgar."

"I know you love it."

Cedric slipped two fingers under the collar. And with a surprisingly strong grip, held Aidan in place.

"That, and everything else."

"Charmer..."

Aidan's smile was calm. Secure. He couldn't be happier.

As the cabin lights flickered, the end of the night was slowly arriving. But that was only the beginning of Aidan's new and somewhat unconventional lifestyle.

With Cedric, only great experiences lay in wait.

"Now. Make the rest of the world disappear."